Bus

the Very Shy Dog

More Adventures
with Phoebe

by **Lisze Bechtold**

Green Light Readers
HOUGHTON MIFFLIN HARCOURT
Boston New York

For information about permission to reproduce selections from this book,
write to trade.permissions@hmhco.com or to Permissions, Houghton Mifflin Harcourt
Publishing Company, 3 Park Avenue, 19th Floor, New York, New York 10016.

hmhco.com

The text of this book is set in 17-point Goudy.
The illustrations are ink and watercolor on paper.

The Library of Congress Cataloging-in-Publication data is on file for
Buster the Very Shy Dog and *Buster & Phoebe: The Great Bone Game.*

ISBN: 978-1-328-90022-7 GLR paperback
ISBN: 978-1-328-90090-6 GLR paper over board

Manufactured in China
SCP 10 9 8 7 6 5 4 3 2 1

4500693307

CONTENTS

Bone Finding

Buster liked to hide his bones in secret places.
But it was hard to find them again.
And when he did find one,
Phoebe often said it was hers.

"How do you know?" asked Buster.
"Well, um, it has my special teeth marks,"
said Phoebe.
I need special teeth marks, too, thought Buster.
He practiced making special teeth marks.

A few days later,
some men began to dig in the yard.
"Look!" cried Phoebe.
"They're finding our bones!"
Phoebe barked and barked,
but the men did not go away.

They wheeled in a big machine.
They shoveled sand into it and added water.
It turned around and around, growling loudly.
"It's going to eat our bones!" cried Phoebe.
"But if we go out there," said Buster,
"it might eat us."

Phoebe barked at the machine all afternoon.
"Has it eaten any of our bones yet?" asked Buster.
"Not any of *my* bones," said Phoebe.
Buster peeked out.

The men took gray mud out of the machine
and put it around the hole.
Then they put bricks on top of the mud.
"How will we get our bones?" cried Buster.
"We can't dig through bricks!"

Finally, the men went away.
"Let's go!" said Phoebe.

But the dog door was locked.
"You can't go out until the cement dries,"
said Roger.

Buster and Phoebe watched the cement dry.
It took a very long time.

At last Roger opened the door.
They raced out into the cool evening air.
"Here is one of my bones!" cried Phoebe.
"And another!"
Soon she had a big pile.

Buster looked and looked.
"Where are *my* bones?" he asked.
"The machine must have eaten them," said Phoebe.
Buster looked some more.

At last he found one.
"Hurray!" he cried. "Oh . . . but this is one
of your bones, Phoebe."

She looked at him with surprise.
"How do you know?" she asked.

"My bones have a special chew mark," said Buster.
"Like that one . . . and that one.
Hey! You have *my* bones!"

"No I don't!" said Phoebe.
"Yes you do," said Buster.
"My bones have an X.
Your bones do not!"

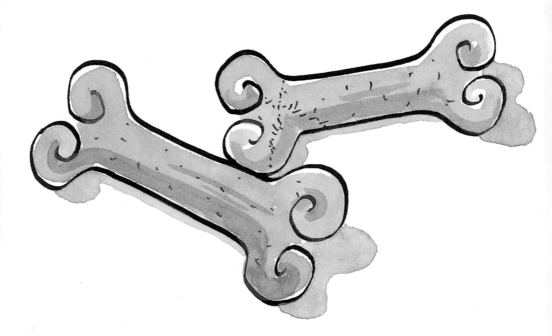

Phoebe looked at the bones.
"Now I won't be rich anymore," she whined.

They sorted the bones into two piles.
"Look," said Buster. "Now we're *both* rich."
"For now . . ." said Phoebe.

Buster and Phoebe
Meet the Garbage Bandit

One night something dug through the garbage cans.
The next morning Roger said, "What a mess.
Buster! Phoebe! Bad dogs!
No biscuits for you two today!"

"We didn't do it!" barked Phoebe.

"I want my biscuit."

But Roger did not understand.

"Phoebe," said Buster, "if we catch the garbage bandit, then Roger will know we didn't do it."

"And I can get my biscuit," added Phoebe.

After supper Buster and Phoebe hid
near the garbage cans and kept watch.
Late into the night Buster heard a sound.
Skitch, skitch, skitch.
"Phoebe, listen!" he said.
"I don't hear anything," she said.
Skitch, skitch, skitch.
"There it is again," said Buster.
"Do you hear it now?"
"No!" said Phoebe. "Now be quiet."
Phoebe doesn't hear very well, thought Buster.

He squinted into the darkness.
A dark shape waddled across the lawn.

"The Garbage Bandit!" cried Buster.
He jumped up. "BARK ARK ARK ARK ARK!"
"Buster! Wait!" cried Phoebe.
"Can't you see it's a . . .

SKUNK?!"

But it was too late.

The skunk turned and raised its tail.

Buster yelped and leapt back.

His eyes stung.
He rubbed his nose on the grass.
"Pew-ee! You stink!" said Phoebe.

"Pew-ee! You stink!" said Roger.
"Come on, you need a tomato juice bath."

"You don't see very well," said Phoebe.
"Let *me* catch the Garbage Bandit."

The next night
Buster watched Phoebe
try to catch the Garbage Bandit.

But Phoebe did not catch the Garbage Bandit.

"You didn't *hear* him," said Buster.
"And you didn't *see* him!" said Phoebe.
"I think," said Buster, "it will take my good ears *and* your good eyes to catch the bandit."

That night Buster listened with his good ears and Phoebe watched with her good eyes.

They did not catch the skunk.

They did not catch the cats.
But they *did* catch . . .

the Garbage Bandits—all three of them!

"Good job, Buster and Phoebe!" said Roger.

Now both Buster and Phoebe
guard Roger's house.
They guard it from
everything Phoebe sees . . .

And they guard it from everything Buster hears.